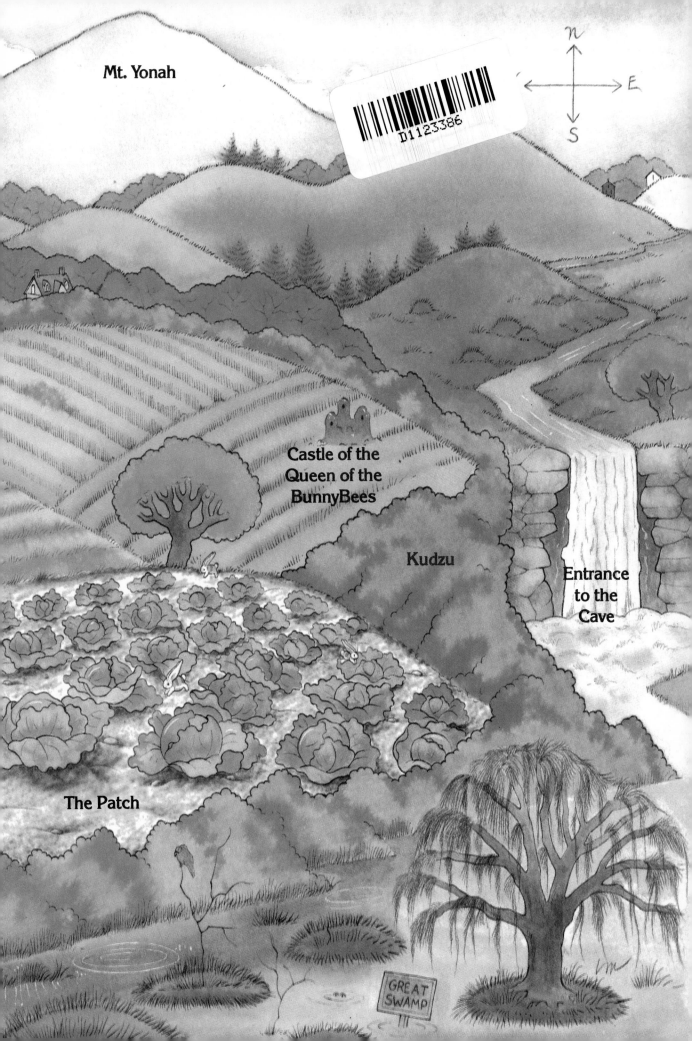

Copyright © 1984 Original Appalachian Artworks, Inc. Published in the United States by Parker Brothers, Division of CPG Products Corp. Cabbage Patch Kids™ and the character names contained in this book are trademarks of and licensed from Original Appalachian Artworks, Inc. Cleveland, GA. U.S.A. All rights reserved.

Library of Congress Cataloging in Publication Data: Robinson, Marileta. The big bicycle race. (Cabbage Patch kids). SUMMARY: The Cabbage Patch kids celebrate the Fourth of July with a picnic and a bicycle race that has a surprise winner.
[1. Bicycle racing—Fiction.   2. Picnicking—Fiction]   I. Morrill, Leslie, ill.   II. Title.   III. Series.
PZ7.R56747Bi   1984   [E]   83-26261   ISBN 0-910313-29-6
Manufactured in the United States of America   1 2 3 4 5 6 7 8 9 0

The
Big Bicycle Race

Story by Marileta Robinson
Pictures by Leslie Morrill

Sybil Sadie was standing guard at the secret entrance to the Cabbage Patch. Suddenly, she clapped her hands and jumped up and down.

"He's coming, y'all! I hear him! Xavier's coming!" The Cabbage Patch Kids dropped what they were doing and came running.

In a moment, a boy gently pushed his way through the vine-covered entrance and found himself staring into a ring of smiling faces.

"Hey, Xavier," shouted the 'Kids, all trying to hug him at once.

"Hey," said Xavier with a grin.

"Tell us a story, Xavier," said Ramie, grabbing his hand and pulling him toward a large, shady oak tree at the edge of the Cabbage Patch.

"I'll do better than that," said Xavier. He sat down with his back against the tree. The others crowded around him as close as they could. "I'll tell you about some real-life goings on. You ever hear of a down-home party?"

The 'Kids shook their heads. "That's some kind of a get-together when all the kinfolk gather, isn't it?" asked Tyler Bo.

Xavier grinned. "That's right, it is. They pack picnic lunches and play games and have races."

"I like the picnic part!" said Will Henry, who was always hungry.

"I like the racing part!" said Sybil Sadie. "With prizes!"

Georgia Ann said quietly, "I like the part about families. Wouldn't it be nice to have a mother and father?"

The others nodded and smiled. They each wanted a real family as badly as she did.

"Xavier," she said, "couldn't we have a down-home party here? It would be a lot of fun, and . . . and it would be almost like being part of a family."

Suddenly, all the 'Kids were shouting at once. "Oh, Xavier, could we, please? Could we?"

"Sure," said Xavier. "That's a wonderful idea."

"What kind of race could we have, Xavier?" said Tyler Bo.

"Well, there are foot races, sack races, three-legged races, bike races . . ."

"A bike race! That's it!" The other children nodded excitedly. They loved riding bikes as much as birds love flying.

"Sounds like you're all set," said Xavier. "I'd better be getting home before my aunt and uncle worry about me."

"But you'll come back for our party, won't you, Xavier?" asked Bobbie Jean.

"You bet, and I'll bring a special surprise for you all." The children gave Xavier another hug, and he slipped back through the vines.

"Let's get to work," said Bobbie Jean. "We'll need to make a list of the kinds of sandwiches we want for the picnic."

":Peanut butter and strawberry jam," said Rebecca Ruby.

"Bananas and honey," said Will Henry. "Yum yum!"

"Ugh!" said Baby Dodd.

When several kinds of sandwiches had been added to the list, Otis Lee said, "Let's go over to the Castle of the Queen of the BunnyBees and tell her about the race!"

They met the Queen of the BunnyBees in the castle throne room. "It's a delightful idea," she said when she had heard their plans. "Please let me donate a prize for the winner of the race. Tied to the old pine tree at the edge of the 'Patch you will find a pony. That will be the prize."

Sybil Sadie's eyes grew wide as she thought about the pony. How beautiful she would look as she rode the pony around the Cabbage Patch! She and Otis Lee were the fastest riders in the group. With luck, she could win. But a quick look at Otis Lee told her he was thinking the same thing.

"We'd better start practicing," she said.

"Yippee!" shouted the others. They ran outside the castle to get their bikes.

On her way out, Georgia Ann saw Dawson Glen standing by himself with his hands stuck in his pockets.

"Why, what's the matter, Dawson Glen?" she said. "You look sadder than a frog without a pond."

"Aw, nothing," said Dawson Glen. "Only I know I can't ride as fast as the other 'Kids can. And my bike is all beat up from me falling over so much. I might as well not even enter the old race!"

Dawson Glen kicked at a pebble and walked slowly away.

Sybil Sadie came out, pushing her bike. "What's the matter with Dawson Glen?" she asked.

Georgia Ann told her what Dawson Glen had said. "We ought to help him learn to ride," she added.

Sybil Sadie frowned. "Not me," she said. "I'll have to practice myself if I'm going to win that pony."

Otis Lee came out chuckling. "You ought to see Dawson Glen's bike," he said. "It looks like it's been in a fight with a bulldozer!"

"Couldn't we help him fix it up?" said Georgia Ann.

"Not me," said Otis Lee. "I've got to work on my own bike if I'm going to win that race." He grinned at Sybil Sadie.

"Well, I'm going to help him," said Georgia Ann, and she rode off to find Dawson Glen.

The next day, the Cabbage Patch Kids were whizzing up and down every path in the valley, practicing for the big race.

Georgia Ann picked Dawson Glen up from the ground and brushed the dirt off him. "Let's try it again," she said. "You almost got it that time. Just remember to keep your balance."

Otis Lee went zooming by. He was feeling good because he just knew that he would win the race, but when he looked over his shoulder and saw Dawson Glen sprawled in the dust, he felt a little less happy. Maybe he should have given Dawson Glen a little bit of help.

As she sped down a hill, Sybil Sadie could almost see herself riding the pony. How wonderful she would look on it as she pranced around the Cabbage Patch. Then she glanced over and saw Dawson Glen trudging up a hill, pushing his bike. A little, tight knot started to form in her stomach.

"It's no use, Georgia Ann," said Dawson Glen. "We've been practicing all day and I still can't make it to the bottom of the hill without falling off. And anyway, my bike's in no shape for the race."

"I know," said Georgia Ann. "If I could only find a wrench, maybe we could fix it. We just can't give up!"

"Would this help?"

Georgia Ann and Dawson Glen looked around in surprise. There stood Otis Lee, holding out a wrench.

"I got to thinking," he said. "No race and no pony is worth it if it makes me act ugly to my friends."

"That goes for me too," said Sybil Sadie, smiling behind Otis Lee. "Now, Dawson Glen, you come with me. You're going to wear out poor Georgia Ann. Besides, I know some tricks that might help you."

"And I'll see what I can do with this bike," said Otis Lee. "I'm afraid it's going to take more than a wrench, though."

For the rest of the week, all the Cabbage Patch Kids took turns helping Dawson Glen.
Then they helped Bobbie Jean make food for the party.

At last the day arrived — the day of the down-home party.
Xavier came early, carrying a big, wooden tub with a
strange-looking contraption on the top, which he said was an
ice cream maker for the picnic.

The last event of the day was the Bike Race. The Cabbage Patch Kids lined up their bikes at the starting line.

Colonel Casey climbed up on a stump and raised his wing for attention.

"Now, I reckon y'all know the rules for this race," he said. "Three times around the Cabbage Patch, and the first one to finish is the winner. If you fall off, get back on your bike and keep a-going."

Several 'Kids looked at Dawson Glen, who blushed and grinned.

"And y'all know what the prize is — the wonderful pony donated by our friend, the Queen of the BunnyBees."

Otis Lee and Sybil Sadie looked at each other and tightened their grips on their handlebars.

"All right now, on your marks, get set, GO!"

A cloud of dust rose as the riders took off. When it settled, Otis Lee saw that he was in the lead. Ducking his head into the wind, he pedaled as hard as he could. He could hear the other bikes getting closer, but he crossed the line ahead of the others.

"Two more laps to go!" called Colonel Casey.

Sybil Sadie's braids were flying straight out behind her as she crossed the line. Otis Lee was just ahead of her, hunched over his bike. She could hear the hum of his wheels. Leaning forward, she took a deep breath and began to pedal steadily, faster and faster. By the time they reached the starting line the second time, she was in the lead.

"One more lap!" called Colonel Casey.

Dawson Glen had started the race next to Georgia Ann. He didn't expect to win, but he was happy he could keep up with the others. Then to his surprise, he pulled ahead of Georgia Ann and the other racers, one by one.

Now he was in third place. The wind blew in his face, and the trees zipped by. He felt as if he were flying.

Now he was even with Otis Lee.

Now he was catching up with Sybil Sadie.

Zoom! He crossed the finish line.

"The winner!" shouted Colonel Casey. "Dawson Glen!"

The Queen of the BunnyBees was waiting in her throne room.

"The prize goes to Dawson Glen," she said. Then she smiled at the 'Kids. "But I'm very proud of all of you."

When Otis Lee imagined Dawson Glen riding on the pony, he felt very disappointed, but if anyone had to beat him, he was glad that it was Dawson Glen. After all, hadn't he helped him fix up the winning bike?

When Sybil Sadie thought about Dawson Glen riding on the pony, she felt a small tear form at the corner of her eye. She wiped it away and smiled. If anyone had to beat her, she was glad it was Dawson Glen. After all, hadn't she helped coach the winning rider?

Dawson Glen whispered to the Queen. She nodded and smiled.

"Dawson Glen wants me to announce that he will not keep the pony for himself. He wants all the rest of you 'Kids to care for it, ride it, and love it, too."

"Hooray for Dawson Glen!" shouted Sybil Sadie.

"Hooray for Dawson Glen!" shouted Otis Lee.

"Hooray for Dawson Glen!" cheered all the Cabbage Patch Kids.

Then Will Henry shouted, "Let's eat!" and everyone cheered again.

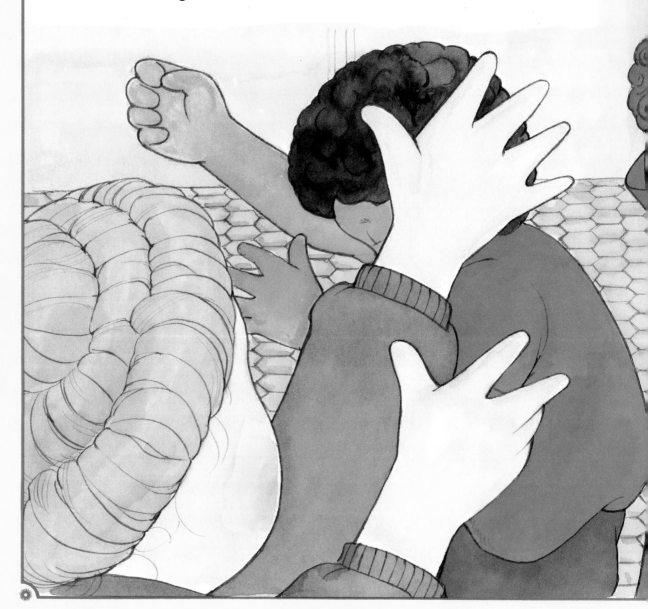

After the 'Kids had eaten and enjoyed the delicious ice cream Xavier made, they all went to find the pony.
Sybil Sadie fed it an apple, and all the 'Kids admired it.

Finally, they all lay back to watch the clouds turn pink over the Cabbage Patch.

"It's been a wonderful down-home party," thought Georgia Ann. She smiled down at Baby Dodd, who had fallen asleep in her lap. "A real family celebration."

Blue Hole

The
Gold Mine

Kudzu

Lavendar's
House